Rookie reader®

What Good Is a Tree?

By Larry Dane Brimner

Illustrated by Leo Landry

Children's Press®
A Division of Scholastic Inc.
New York • Toronto • London • Auckland • Sydney
Mexico City • New Delhi • Hong Kong
Danbury, Connecticut

For Dana Rau
—L. D. B.
For my parents
—L. L.

Reading Consultant
Linda Cornwell
Learning Resource Consultant
Indiana Department of Education

Library of Congress Cataloging-in-Publication Data
Brimner, Larry Dane.
   What good is a tree? / by Larry Dane Brimner;
illustrated by Leo Landry.
      p. cm. — (Rookie reader)
   Summary: When a boy wonders, "What good is a
tree?" he and his sister come up with a lot of
answers, from using it as a fort to making it second
base.
   ISBN 0-516-20953-1
   [1. Trees—Fiction. 2. Stories in rhyme.]
I. Landry, Leo, ill. II. Title. III. Series.
PZ7.B767Wh 1998
[E]—dc21   97-40053
                                        CIP
                                        AC

"Look! A tree."

"Big deal! What good is a tree?"

4

"What good is
a tree?" I said.
"You're kidding me!

A tree reaches high.

It holds up the sky.

It is a fort or a castle,

and from it, we can spy.

13

A tree is second base.

The end of the race.

Need a place to hide?

It can be a rocket to space.

21

See that spruce?

23

It might be a bear,
or maybe a moose.

24

Maybe it's a jail,

but we'll get loose.

What good is a tree?
Oh, big brother, don't you see?"

31

Word List (57 Words)

a	end	jail	place	the
and	fort	kidding	race	to
base	from	look	reaches	tree
be	get	loose	rocket	up
bear	good	maybe	said	we
big	hide	me	second	we'll
brother	high	might	see	what
but	holds	moose	sky	you
can	I	need	space	you're
castle	is	of	spruce	
deal	it	oh	spy	
don't	it's	or	that	

About the Author

Larry Dane Brimner has written many Rookie Readers, including *Lightning Liz, Dinosaurs Dance, Aggie and Will,* and *Nana's Hog.* Mr. Brimner is also the author of *E-mail* and *The World Wide Web* for Children's Press. He lives in the southwest region of the United States.

About the Illustrator

Leo Landry lives in Boston, Massachusetts with his wife, Mary, and his daughter, Sophie (who posed for some of the illustrations in this book). This is his first book for children.